Angelina Ballerina™
Tries Again

Based on the stories by Katharine Holabird
Based on the illustrations by Helen Craig

Ready-to-Read

Simon Spotlight
New York   London   Toronto   Sydney   New Delhi

SIMON SPOTLIGHT
An imprint of Simon & Schuster Children's Publishing Division
1230 Avenue of the Americas, New York, New York 10020
This Simon Spotlight edition May 2020
Illustrations by Mike Deas
© 2020 Helen Craig Ltd. and Katharine Holabird.
The Angelina Ballerina name and character and the dancing Angelina logo are trademarks
of HIT Entertainment Limited, Katharine Holabird, and Helen Craig.
All rights reserved, including the right of reproduction in whole or in part in any form.
SIMON SPOTLIGHT, READY-TO-READ, and colophon are registered trademarks of Simon & Schuster, Inc.
For information about special discounts for bulk purchases, please contact Simon & Schuster Special Sales at
1-866-506-1949 or business@simonandschuster.com.
Manufactured in the United States of America 0320 LAK
10 9 8 7 6 5 4 3 2 1
ISBN 978-1-5344-6446-9 (hc)
ISBN 978-1-5344-6445-2 (pb)
ISBN 978-1-5344-6447-6 (eBook)

Note to Readers: In this book, we use the word *twirl* in place of *pirouette* (SAY: pir-OH-wet). Pirouette is a ballet term that means spinning around on one foot balanced on toes. Professional ballet dancers can typically do four to five pirouettes in a row.

Angelina loved dancing
with her friends at
Miss Lilly's Ballet School.

One day Miss Lilly smiled and said, "I have some exciting news! We will be dancing *Sleeping Mouseling* at the Royal Palace!"

"Angelina will dance
the lead part,"
Miss Lilly continued.
"Practice begins tomorrow!"

"Ooooh, I am so happy!"
Angelina said.

After class,
Angelina shared her
good news with her family.

"This calls for a slice
of cheddar cheese pie!"
her father cheered.

Over the next week, all the little dancers practiced the dance for *Sleeping Mouseling* with Miss Lilly.

Angelina was working hard, but she kept getting dizzy trying to do a double twirl.

"You can do it, Angelina!"
William cheered.

Angelina's best friend,
Alice, cheered her on too.

But Angelina just
could not
do double twirls
without getting
dizzy.

Angelina went home upset
every night after
ballet class.
"Maybe I should give up,"
she cried to her mom.

"Do not worry.
Just try your best,"
Mrs. Mouseling said,
comforting her.

The next day, Angelina
tried again . . .

and down she fell again!

Alice gave her a hug. "You just need more practice," she said. "You will get it soon!"

Angelina bravely kept on
practicing.
She tried doing
double twirls again
and again.

And then she tried
some more.

Finally, Angelina landed
her double twirl!

Angelina was very proud,
but would she be able
to do it at the show?

Soon it was the day
of the show.

Angelina took her place
on stage and began to
dance.

Soon it was time
for Angelina
to do her double twirl.

Angelina twirled.
Then she twirled again!
She did it!
She did not get dizzy!
She did not fall!

Everyone cheered loudly,
especially the Princess of
Mouseland.

"I am so glad I kept trying!"
Angelina said,
doing a lovely curtsy
for the Princess.